About the Author

Roger Flavell is a musician and song-writer. In his professional career he has been involved with a variety of chart-topping bands and has worked with many well-known artistes. This children's book is his first published work and he hopes very much that you will enjoy the stories.

To Keegan and Kelsey
Very best wishes

Roger Flower.

The Adventures of
Colonel Crunch and Friends

Roger Flavell

Illustrations by David Ashton

The Adventures of Colonel Crunch and Friends

Nightingale Books

A CIP catalogue record for this title is
available from the British Library.
ISBN 978-1-83875-258-3

Nightingale Books is an imprint of
Pegasus Elliot MacKenzie Publishers Ltd.

www.pegasuspublishers.com

Nightingale Books
Sheraton House Castle Park
Cambridge England

First Published in 2021

Printed & Bound in Great Britain

Acknowledgements

To Jennifer Miles Secretarial for her typing work.
To Tex Marsh for a conceptual idea.
To my illustrator, David Ashton, for his hard work.
To my family for their patience and support.

Contents

A Slight Explosion

In the incredibly sleepy village of Lower Hillstock,
there was not a great deal happening on this
particular day. It was a Monday morning and there
was still a light mist in the air although it was almost
eleven thirty. Usually, by this time in November,
the sun had managed to break through to reveal
the hills and the surrounding countryside.

Everything in the vicinity was incredibly quiet, as you would expect in this part of the world, until there was an almighty sound of a blast which seemed to come from the big red barn at the farm. All the birds took to the air following this sound. And then you could see a column of smoke rising up into the air and disappearing into the mist.

Farmer James, who had not long since returned from checking on his sheep up on the hills, came rushing out of the old farmhouse and was now running towards the barn. What he saw next greatly surprised him. It was the figure of Colonel Crunch, covered in soot and holding his ears, staggering out of the big open doors.

"Goodness gracious me," said Farmer James. "What on earth has been going on here?" At which point another figure came reeling out of the now diminishing smoke. It was Professor Blenkinsop, also known as Professor Bubbles, whose curly hair on the sides of his bald head was literally smouldering. Farmer James grabbed a metal pail of water which was near the cattle drinking trough and threw it over the professor's head.

"Ah, that's better," said the Professor. "Thank you very much, it was getting a wee bit warm in there!" Colonel Crunch, in his now rather tattered jacket, was patting his clothing and rubbing his eyes.

"That was a close call, Bubbles," he exclaimed.
"We didn't expect that to happen!" The very wet
professor looked at him and said, "I think that we might
have got the explosive mixture slightly wrong.
I'll have to do some more calculations."
"You most certainly will!" replied the colonel.

Farmer James had allowed them to use the barn,
but he certainly wanted to know what they were doing
in there. He didn't want to lose his precious barn.
"What were you doing in there today?"
he asked them in a very stern voice.

"Just working on a new propulsion mixture for our rocket," replied Crunch. "A ROCKET...?" shouted the farmer. "Why indeed are you trying to build a rocket?" Colonel Crunch and Professor Bubbles looked at him and at the same time said, "So that we can blast off into space and land back again in the same place." "We have got it all planned out, you know," said Crunch enthusiastically.

Farmer James shook his head in disbelief and also wagged his finger at them, saying, "You can go into space whenever you like, but try not to take my barn with you next time!"

A Large Parachute

Colonel Crunch had been in the army many years ago and in that time he had made a few parachute jumps.

He liked all the activities to do with the air, maybe that is why he wanted to build a rocket ship.

Anyway, it came to the front of his mind that he would really like to do one more parachute jump. "Just for old times' sake," he thought to himself. "Maybe someone else might like to accompany me." And he wondered who might be willing to go with him.

Crunch went round the village asking people but nobody at all seemed to be the slightest bit interested in this hair-brained scheme. Mind you, it didn't really help matters when he approached folk and asked them if they fancied 'getting their knees in the breeze'.

"What on earth are you talking about!" replied Reverend Ken Ardley, the local vicar. "I am asking you if you would like to make a parachute jump with me," said the colonel. "Not at all," replied the vicar. "I'd rather keep my feet on solid ground, thank you!"

EASTON-ON-THE-WOLD

By this time, it was obvious to Crunch that he was on his own and so he set about organising himself for the task ahead. He drove over to Easton-on-the-Wold, which was an air force camp not very far away, where he knew some of the staff. He arrived at the camp gates and asked if he could see Sergeant Bulliman, a parachuting instructor. They had crossed paths before.

The sergeant was pleased to see the colonel and listened to his request and asked him if he was in good health. "Of course I'm in good health. Fit as a fiddle, don't you know!" said Crunch. "Very well then, come back next Monday and I will train you up and we will get you in the air," said the sergeant.

The colonel was over the moon with this and arrived back at the airfield early on the next Monday. Sergeant Bulliman, who was a stickler for the rules, put Crunch through his paces. He had him dangling in a harness, he had him jumping off a box onto the floor, he had him counting out aloud. The old colonel was still enthusiastic, although a little tired by now.

The sergeant had arranged the drop from the aircraft for late afternoon that day, all being well. He kitted up both of them with their parachutes and they made their way out to the small aeroplane.

"No going back now. It's crunch-time!" thought the colonel as they climbed aboard.

The little aircraft climbed quickly to the designated height and Sergeant Bulliman indicated to the colonel that he should shuffle towards the open door and checked the static line which would automatically open Crunch's parachute when he left the aircraft. "In the door," shouted the sergeant very loudly.

 "GO," he bawled at the top of his voice and the colonel threw himself out into the slipstream!

"One thousand... two thousand... three thousand... four thousand..." screamed Crunch, at which point he was enormously pleased to see a very large green parachute opening above his head. "Marvellous," said Crunch, now silently floating through the air. The only problem was that the wind had slightly increased and he was at this point in time flying towards a little wood on the edge of the airfield. There was not a lot that he could do except keep his feet and knees together and keep his elbows in and his head down!

The branches came up to meet him at quite a pace, but somehow the parachute caught on a branch and there was the colonel totally unhurt but dangling about ten feet off the ground. "Marvellous," said Crunch smiling to himself.

"We'll soon get you down, sir," said some of the airmen who had raced across the airfield in a jeep with a ladder on board.

Crunch was safe and had achieved what he had set out to do. He had once again made a parachute jump.

The Combine Harvester

It was now towards the end of summer and thoughts at the surrounding farms were turning towards harvesting all the crops. The fields of corn and barley and wheat were golden and very soon they would need to be cut and to be gathered in.

Colonel Crunch had heard that Farmer Stubbleton had bought a brand new combine harvester and he was keen to get over there to see what this machine could do and indeed to watch it in action.
As you know the colonel was very interested in machines of every shape and every description.

He made his way over to Stubbleton Farm which, as the crow flies, was really only just a couple of miles. Crunch arrived to see the farmer tinkering with some of the equipment in the yard and he shouted over to him.
"Good day, Mr. Stubbleton, how are you?"

STUBBLETON FARM

"Very well, thank you," replied the farmer who was dressed in an old green boiler suit.

"To what do I owe this pleasure, Colonel?" Crunch told him that he had come over especially to look at the brand new combine harvester. "Good timing then," said Mr. Stubbleton. "I am just about to take it out into the first field of wheat that needs to be cut."

"Marvellous idea," replied the colonel who was now following in the farmer's footsteps. And as they walked around the corner there in front of them was this huge red machine which towered over them.

"I bet that cost you a pretty penny!" said Crunch.
"You can say that again!" said Mr. Stubbleton.
"I bet that cost you a pretty penny!" said Crunch one more
time. The farmer rolled his eyes and smiled as he invited
Crunch aboard his new machine.

They had to climb up the ladder at the side in order to get
into the large cab at the front. "You sit in the seat on the
left and I will sit over here on the right," said the farmer
who started up the motor.

Crunch was amazed because it almost looked like the flight deck of an aircraft. There were controls everywhere and a computer screen with lots of information on it. It had heated leather seats and a mini refrigerator under the co-pilot's seat.

"All mod cons," said the farmer who was about to harvest the first row of wheat. He had set the navigation system so that the combine would automatically keep to a straight line. "It is a very clever piece of machinery with state-of-the-art controls," said Mr. Stubbleton. He looked as if he was very proud of this new bit of kit. Crunch was very impressed with it.

"Now, if you like, in a little while I might just let you get into the driver's seat. Would you like to have a go?" said Mr. Stubbleton.

Colonel Crunch was in his element today. "Marvellous!" he said as he sat and watched his friend, Farmer Stubbleton, drive up and down the very large wheat field at the same time controlling the speed of the cutters and the amount that was being loaded into the accompanying truck which collected and then took away the grain when it was full.

"Now it is your turn. We will change seats and you can have a go..." shouted Mr. Stubbleton over the noise of the motor. The Colonel pushed the lever gently and away they went cutting the next swathe of the crop. "Not too fast now!" he shouted to Crunch who was enjoying every second of his new adventure. They got to the end of that row and turned slowly to once again come back up the field.

"You will make a farmer yet," said Stubbleton. "I am not sure about that...!" replied Crunch. "But I tell you what... I will remember this experience for a very long time to come. Marvellous!"

Thinking Cap

Professor Bubbles and the colonel were scratching their heads wondering what kind of a plan they could come up with next. In fact, there wasn't a day that went by when they weren't thinking about possible inventions.

There were all sorts of bits and pieces in the barn that belonged to Farmer James, which they referred to as their 'laboratory'. It had shelves and boxes full of stuff such as screws, cogs, test-tubes, microscopes and telescopes and of course all manner of tools in racks. There were all sorts of materials from metals, plastics, wood, stone and glass. They probably had nearly every material known to man.

Sometimes they asked their other friends if there was anything that they could make that could make their lives easier in some way or other. Mrs. Dorothy Dingley, who owned the little shop in the village, often had an idea. Her friends knew her as Dot. But nine times out of ten her ideas didn't appeal to the inventors.

"Do you remember that time," said Crunch, "when Dot asked us if we could invent a left-handed corkscrew! She thought that it would sell like hot cakes in her shop!"

The pair of them laughed sheepishly because in actual fact they had actually worked on that particular idea for a little while, only to realize that there was probably not a lot of mileage in a left-handed corkscrew! "However, any idea is a good idea. At least it had been an idea!" said the professor scratching his head again. They would just have to keep their thinking caps on.

"That's a great idea," said Crunch. "Let's invent a thinking cap." "Yes," exclaimed Bubbles excitedly. "It would be a device that you put on your head in order to make you think better!" He wished that they had invented it before because it would have made their lives much easier. The colonel agreed, stroking his chin. "We will definitely work on that as soon as possible." They wrote it down in their notebook of 'Possible Projects' and said that they would sleep on it and come back to it the next day.

When Crunch arrived at the laboratory the following day he found that the professor was already there and was busy getting on with the new project. He had found an old metal colander which it seems he was adapting to its new role.

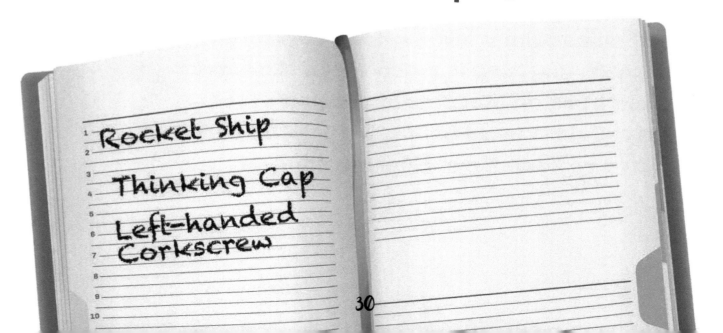

1 Rocket Ship
2
3 Thinking Cap
4
5 Left-handed
6 Corkscrew
7
8
9
10

The colonel saw that there were wires attached to the holes in the colander and he asked if he could help in any way. "Yes, try and find me some small batteries that work," replied Bubbles. He told Crunch that he was in the process of adapting a mini relay switch device that should in theory send very small random currents of electrical charge all around this metal cap.

"Ah," said Crunch enthusiastically. "You mean that this might stimulate the thinking process when it is worn on the head? But who can we try it out on?" They considered this for a minute and decided that they might ask young Tommy, the farm-hand, who was generally not known for coming up with any great thoughts.

"Yes, we will try it out on him just as soon as I have the finished article," said Bubbles as he continued to connect up all the wiring. "It will be safe, won't it?" asked the colonel. "Of course," replied Bubbles who told the colonel that there would only ever be a tiny amount of voltage in each impulse.

After a couple of hours, around about lunch-time, they asked young Tommy if he could spare a few minutes to help them with an experiment.

"What do you want me to do?" said the young farm-hand slightly bemused.

"We would like you to wear this 'Thinking Cap' on your head to see if you can come up with any bright ideas." "Oh, right..." said Tommy who didn't like thinking too much.

They sat him down and placed the device on his head. Bubbles busied himself with the equipment and when he was ready he said, "I am going to switch it on now. See if you have any great thoughts that suddenly pop into your mind. Here we go," and he switched it on. Various lights went on and off in no particular order until suddenly Tommy's face lit up with a beam and he shouted out,

"Invisible Paint!"

The professor immediately switched off the 'Thinking Cap' and he and the colonel shouted with one voice, "It works... the 'Thinking Cap' works!"

"Well done, Tommy. What a brilliant idea, Invisible Paint! We will start work on it as soon as possible!"

"Extraordinary," said Crunch who was as pleased as punch with the outcome of their latest experiment.

Invisible Paint

It had been a while since that experiment with their 'Thinking Cap' when Tommy the farm-hand had come up with bright idea of 'Invisible Paint'. Colonel Crunch and Professor Bubbles Blenkinsop were looking through their notebook of possible ideas and decided that they would probably try and make some headway with this plan.

Professor Bubbles needed to think deeply about this because it was not going to be an easy task to create some 'Invisible Paint'. Not that the paint itself would be invisible, but when the paint was applied to an object then that object would disappear! And for how long would the object remain invisible? As yet he was not quite sure!

The colonel and the professor spent a long time discussing the various possibilities of this experiment and they made a lot of notes on how this could be achieved.

"We need to think outside the box!" said the colonel. "You can say that again," said the professor. "We need to think outside the box!" repeated the colonel. "Very funny," replied Bubbles who did not have quite the same sense of humour and was far more serious than Crunch.

But it was not too long after that when the professor said that he thought that the colonel had actually given him the seed of an idea. "A box, a glass box with a lid. Yes, that might be the way forward," said Bubbles enthusiastically, whilst rubbing his head at the same time.

The colonel asked him why they might need a glass container. Bubbles was now on a roll and was beginning to tell Crunch about the plan that was formulating in his brain. His idea was that an amount of luminous paint would be put inside the glass container and then be bombarded with a beam of laser light. The professor thought that this would excite the luminous paint inside the glass vessel and change the granular structure of the light molecules of the paint.

At which point, when this modified paint was applied to an object, then at least for a while light could not be reflected back from the object and therefore that object would appear to disappear!

"That is my theory anyway," said Bubbles waving his arms in the air. And the colonel agreed that it was a splendid idea and that they should have a go at it as soon as possible.

Crunch knew a man who as a lighting engineer not only had access to a variety of lasers, but was willing to lend them whatever they needed. The only condition was that he gave them a safety briefing before letting them have the two hundred to five hundred milliamp laser.

He also lent them two pairs of laser goggles to protect their eyes.

Once they had got all the necessary equipment together in their laboratory in Farmer James' barn, the two of them started work on this experiment. Bubbles explained that they would bombard the luminous paint in the glass container with a beam of laser light of varying intensity in order to see if they might change the property of the paint. They changed the intensity of the laser beam and the amount of time that it bombarded the paint. And immediately after each session they painted an object with the modified luminous paint.

Suddenly they noticed that the pebble that they had just painted seemed to disappear! "We have done it... we have invented invisible paint!" they both shouted.

The colonel thought that he should pour a little of the invisible paint into another container, but in his state of excitement his hands were slightly shaking and some of this liquid spilt onto his right index finger. The finger started to disappear at the very same moment that Professor Bubbles asked him where the pair of tongs were.

"Over There!!!"

said Crunch who was now pointing in the direction of the tongs. But unfortunately Bubbles was unable to see where the colonel was pointing with his now invisible finger!

"Whatever is going to happen?" exclaimed Crunch who naturally was rather worried about his finger that appeared to be missing.
"I can feel it, but I can't see it," he added.

"Don't worry," replied Bubbles reassuringly, who had just noticed that the pebble by now had started to re-appear on the laboratory bench. The professor explained that it had been made invisible but only for a short amount of time after which the luminous paint returned to its original state.

"Your finger will re-appear in no time at all and then you will be able to point at whatever you like," said the professor who was smiling and wagging his right finger at Colonel Crunch.

Play Power

Colonel Crunch had taken his two young grandchildren, Matt and Rosie, after school down to the park in order to have some fun and fresh air. It had been quite busy with a lot of youngsters using all of the rides. After an hour or so it was time to take them home as they were now hungry and tired. He dropped them off at their parents' house and went on his way, back to Lower Hillstock where he lived.

The next day Crunch had arranged to meet Professor Bubbles Blenkinsop at their laboratory to consider the possibilities of work on a new invention. When they got together the colonel told the professor about the splendid time that he had enjoyed with his grandchildren during the previous afternoon at the large park in the local town. "Lots of rides, you know," said Crunch. "All very busy," he added.

"Let's think about that for a minute or two," replied Bubbles who was rubbing his head and stroking his chin which he often did when thinking.

"Yes, there were swings, roundabouts and see-saws. Each one in motion going backwards-and-forwards, round-and-around, and up-and-down," said the colonel.

Bubbles was looking very excited as he considered the various movements of these playground rides. And then the penny dropped!

"We will make some simple generators out of magnets and coils to fit each of these types of rides, so that every time that they are in motion they will be able to produce electricity."

"Each ride could be modified to produce electricity which could be fed into the National Grid, in the same way that wind farms generate power," added Crunch excitedly.

"It could also power lights at the playgrounds so that the rides could be used for a longer period when the days get shorter and the nights get longer. And this means that more electricity will be produced because the rides would be in use for more hours," added the professor enthusiastically.

PROPERTY OF
BUBBLES/CRUNCH LTD

It was at this point that they left their laboratory in the barn and walked into the village where they happened to bump into Mrs. Norah Gladstone who was the leader of the council in the local town. She noticed at once that Crunch and the professor appeared to be very excited and she asked them why they were so animated.

The pair told her all about their possible new invention and Norah was also very excited to learn all about it. The three of them discussed how many playgrounds there must be across the land in every village, town and city, not to mention all the adventure theme parks!

Norah Gladstone thought that it was quite possible that all the children who enjoyed going on playground rides might catch the vision that their activity could generate electricity in a very 'green' way.

"Not only that," said Crunch, "but across the whole world too. Just think how many playgrounds there are in every country that could harness power. It could become a global project with children across the world helping to make our planet 'a greener place'."

"It might even spark a new generation of co-operation across the nations," added Norah Gladstone.

They all agreed that they were definitely on to something big with this new invention.

And so both Colonel Crunch and the professor were very keen to shortly follow up on their idea.

Taking to the Air

Colonel Crunch had been down to the local shop, which, as you might recall, was owned and run by Mrs. Dot Dingley, in order to buy some groceries. It was handier and quicker than going all the way into town. Very soon after he had left the shop carrying his bag of items, he caught sight of an old acquaintance, Tim Woodward, who was affectionately known to his friends as 'Woody'.

Crunch called out to him across the street and Tim turned and waved a greeting to the colonel.

"Haven't seen you for a while," said Woody, shaking hands with Crunch and at the same time asking him how he was doing.

"I am fine," replied Crunch. "Where have you been hiding yourself?" Woody explained to Crunch that he hadn't been around for some while because he had been away flying here, there and everywhere. Tim was an aerobatic pilot and had been involved in aerobatic displays and air races all over the world, but right now he was back at home for a few months.

"How marvellous," said the colonel. "Tell you what we should do, and I did mention this before but we never got around to it, why don't you come over to the air park soon and I will take you up in my aircraft for a quick spin."

As you know, Colonel Crunch was very keen on all things to do with the air. So they made a plan to call each other to arrange a suitable day when the weather would be okay.

Crunch was extremely excited when the day came when he was due to go over to Hibson Air Park to meet Woody. They met up in front of the old control tower and they strolled out to where Woody's small red biplane was parked up.

"You will be sitting in the front and we will both wear parachutes," said Woody as he opened the perspex canopy and lifted out two small parachute rigs, one of which he handed to the colonel, at the same time demonstrating how to use it if the need should arise.

He helped Crunch into the front seat of the aircraft and closed his harness and put on his headset so that they could talk to each other in the air. Then Woody climbed into the rear seat and went through the flight checks, after which he shouted, "CLEAR PROP," and started the engine which roared into life. Woody spoke to the control tower as they taxied out towards the grass runway.

"Are you ready for this, Crunch?" said Woody.
"Yes, ready and willing," replied Crunch and the small aircraft quickly gathered speed and before he knew it they were in the air and climbing swiftly away from the ground.

"Everything all right in the front?" asked Woody as he levelled out the plane and he told Crunch that he would start with a slow barrel roll.

They banked to the right and momentarily Crunch felt that he was hanging upside down until the aircraft completed the roll and they were once again in level flight.

"Put your hand on the stick, Crunch, and bank to the right and then to the left to see how responsive she is," said Woody. And so the Colonel moved the stick to the right and to the left and the small aeroplane moved in both directions. "Marvellous," said Crunch with great excitement.

"I have control. Now I will take the aircraft through some aerobatic manoeuvres, but not too fast because I don't want to make you feel unwell," said Woody. "And we will end up with a loop!"

So they went this way and that in the air, and they ended up doing a loop where they were upside down for a short while. They had been flying for about twenty minutes before it was time to return to the small air park and so Woody gently landed the biplane once more on the grass runway. They taxied back and, finally after his checks, turned off the engine.

"Let's get you out. What did you think of that? I hope that you enjoyed it," said Tim 'Woody' Woodward.

"It was a terrific experience," beamed the colonel. "Yes, I will certainly remember that for a very long time. Thank you very much indeed."

"Maybe we will do it again some other time?" said Woody as they waved and parted company.

A Bit of a Pickle

It was towards the end of the summer months and Colonel Crunch decided that he might go and visit his old friends Sir and Lady Godfrey. They lived at the old Manor House which had a mature walled garden.

When he arrived there he was greeted at the door by both of them and they welcomed him into their beautiful home. "I was hoping that we might go and have a look at the walled garden," said Crunch.

"Why, of course," replied Elizabeth Godfrey. "I am sure that Bill the gardener is still here working away as usual. He does love the garden."

Bill Hook had worked at the Manor House for many a long year and in that time he had kept the garden in a wonderful condition. He grew many types of vegetables and fruit. The colonel greeted Bill who offered to show Crunch around in order to see what was growing. "Marvellous. You do a great job here, Bill," commented the colonel as they walked around.

"Thank you very much, Colonel. I do my best, you know."

As they wandered back through the entrance towards the Manor House, Lady Godfrey and Crunch talked about all the fruit and vegetables that were being grown and what would happen to them.

"The ladies down at the Institute make lots of jams and pickles at this time of year so that we can sell them and raise some funds for certain charities. In fact, we are all meeting up on Wednesday to prepare, cook and make jams, pickles and chutneys. Why don't you come on down and help us for as long as it takes. We will provide an apron for you. Come and get your hands dirty. We can always do with another pair of hands!"

"Well, I'm not sure..." replied Crunch.

"That settles it then," said Elizabeth. "We will see you there at nine o'clock sharp!" The colonel couldn't wriggle out of this one and so he agreed to see them all at the hall on Wednesday morning.

He wondered what he was getting himself in for as he
arrived at the hall on that morning and was greeted
by Elizabeth and her team of ladies from the Institute.
Everything was laid out on the tables and in the kitchen
and Crunch was given an apron to put on.

"I am not sure whether it suits you, but at least it will
protect your clothes," said Elizabeth as she handed the
colonel a floral apron. "Would you be kind enough to peel
this bowl of onions please? We will need them soon when
we start cooking," said Mary Dunne, one of the ladies.

"Not a problem," replied Crunch who did not generally
spend too much time in the kitchen. But it wasn't long
before his eyes were streaming and tears were running
down his cheeks as he peeled the onions.

"Phew," he gasped as the strong fumes from the peeled onions wafted up at him. Meanwhile all the ladies were hard at work preparing all the other ingredients that would be going into making the chutney. As soon as Crunch had finished peeling and dicing up the onions they were whisked away and put into the pan to cook.

"You can have a sit-down and a nice cup of tea now. You look as if you are worn out," said Mary.
"Good idea," replied Crunch who was ready for a break.

The ladies carried on cooking all the ingredients which included tomatoes, sultanas, apples, spices, vinegar and some sugar. The smell of all this cooking was making the colonel rather hungry. Soon everything was ready in the big preserving pan and the glass jars had been heated.

"Perhaps you could help us to put the chutney mixture into the jars, Colonel?" said Elizabeth.

Crunch grabbed one of the small jugs and filled it from the big pan. He grabbed a glass jar and began to pour in the mixture. Unfortunately, the glass jar was rather hotter than he had imagined! Consequently, the chutney mixture went all over the place. Some in the jar, some down the side of the jar and some on the table!

"I seem to be getting in a bit of a pickle!" shouted Crunch. And they all laughed out loud. Anyway, he did get the hang of it and they managed to fill all the jars with the chutney that they would sell, along with their jams, cakes and fruit pies, in order to make some money for their charities. It had all been a novel experience for Colonel Crunch, but as usual he had enjoyed himself.

Half-a-Propeller

Colonel Crunch was taking a walk with his dog, Springer, in the woods near to his home. He loved the quiet of the woodland area and he enjoyed looking at all the plants and the different types of trees which grew there. The cool of the shade and the sun's rays dancing through the leaves fascinated him.

The colonel liked to try and name the woodland plants as he came across them. There were different ferns, foxgloves, sages and red campions to mention just a few.

As they walked along his eyes caught sight of a sycamore seed dropping to the ground. Because of its shape, it twizzled down rather like the blades of a tiny helicopter until it reached the floor. Crunch picked it up and studied it for a minute before putting it in to his jacket pocket. "Interesting, very interesting," he said to himself as they continued on their walk.

The thought of these flying seeds would not leave his mind, so when he met up with Professor Bubbles in a couple of days he immediately brought up the subject.

"Now, look at these sycamore seeds," said the colonel as he reached into one of his pockets and placed them on the palm of his outstretched hand.

"Yes, I know that they fly very well," said Bubbles who was studying them.

"They are almost like half-a-propeller," said Crunch. "So why don't we invent a one-bladed propeller?"

"What could we use it for?" replied the professor who was now scratching his head. He often did this when he was deep in thought. "Let me think about this for a minute or two." It wasn't too long before he grinned and started to explain his idea for a one-bladed propeller wind turbine.

"But they normally have three big blades," said the colonel.

"Ah," replied the professor, "but it is all down to the angle of the blade from its root to its tip as I see it, and how it moves in the airstream... in this case... the wind."

"Maybe it only needs to go halfway round rather than all the way?" said Crunch who was now quite excited at the idea and was stroking his chin.

"In that case we would have to make the blade rotate through one hundred and eighty degrees so that it would once again immediately catch the wind and bring it back the other way again.

"And of course it would repeat the process once it got back to the other side," thought Bubbles.

"A bit like a wind-blown pendulum," noted the colonel.

The professor said that he would start work straight away on a mechanism that would change the axis of the propeller blade time every time that it reached the horizontal position in order to bring it back again through its arc.

"Very much like a pendulum motion then," said Crunch. "And, more importantly, each time that it moves back and forth it will be able to generate some power."

The two of them mulled over the initial design for a couple of days and realised that they could actually have a vertical row of these one-bladed propeller generators, one on top of the other. And the row of them would rotate into the prevailing wind at any given time so as to keep the thrust of the propellers turning whenever there was wind, therefore generating electricity.

They were both very pleased with this new idea which had come from simply watching sycamore seeds twizzling their way to the woodland floor.

"Marvellous," said Colonel Crunch.

The Waterbrella

"What a day," thought Colonel Crunch as he was trying to do his shopping in the pouring rain. He almost collided with Reverend and Mrs Ken Ardley as they were also huddled under an umbrella.

"Raining cats and dogs!" shouted the vicar.

"You can say that again," said Crunch. "Raining cats and dogs," repeated the Vicar as he and his wife shuffled off along the street trying to keep dry.

By the time the colonel had returned home he felt rather damp and for a short while he stood in front of the fireplace in order to dry off and get warm again.

"At least an umbrella keeps most of the rain off you," he thought to himself wistfully. But in a strange way he began to consider that it is also quite a waste of water. And so he decided that he would talk the matter over with Professor Bubbles at the very next opportunity, which happened to be during the following week owing to the fact that Bubbles had been away on a very important scientific conference.

"What is it that you wanted to talk to me about?"
asked the professor when they next met.

"Well, I was wondering what we could do about all
the water that runs off our umbrellas when it is raining.
In a strange way it does seem such a waste,
you know!" mused the colonel.

"Yes, I see what you mean," said the professor who was
beginning to scratch his head as if to encourage another
bright idea. "Mmm... we need to conserve the water,
but at the same time we need to keep ourselves dry!"

It was suddenly so obvious to them both that what was
required was actually a sort of inverted umbrella. So, on the
top part the water could be collected and at the same time
the bottom part would keep the user dry.

"Marvellous," said Crunch and he asked Bubbles
if would be able to start work on a prototype as soon as
possible. Bubbles agreed that because he was back
from the conference he would be able to start to think
about it straight away.

A week later they met up at their laboratory to discuss the progress on their new invention. Sure enough the professor had in that time managed to build a prototype which he unfurled. He explained that the mechanism had been slightly tricky to work out but he had managed to overcome the problem. "Now look," said the colonel, "I have been wondering if we could somehow filter the rain water that is collected?"

"Ah, yes," replied Bubbles. "I somehow knew that you might ask me that.

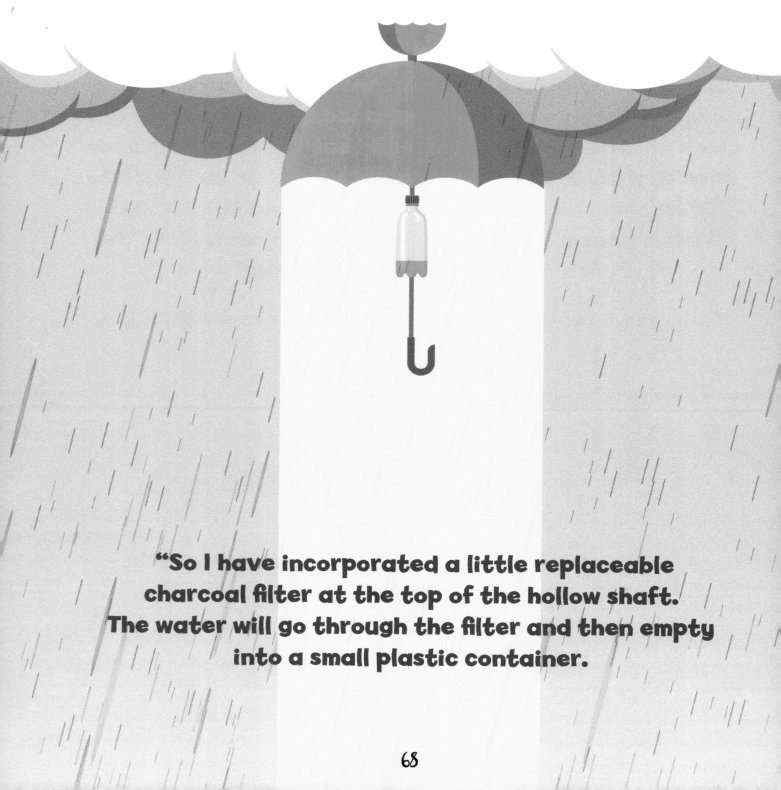

"So I have incorporated a little replaceable charcoal filter at the top of the hollow shaft. The water will go through the filter and then empty into a small plastic container.

"When the container is full of fresh pure water, all that you need to do is unclip it, stow it in your pockets or your backpack, and replace it with an empty container. Easy!"

"A constant supply of drinking water when you have your adapted umbrella. We will have to call it a Waterbrella!" said Colonel Crunch. And they were both very pleased with the result of what they had achieved.

Lightning Source UK Ltd.
Milton Keynes UK
UKHW050702181121
394131UK00005B/42